Lucy's Rabbit

Jennifer Northway

F

FRANCES LINCOLN
CHILDREN'S BOOKS

Jennifer Northway has written and illustrated a number of acclaimed picture books. Her book *Get Lost, Laura!* was shortlisted for the Smarties Award. In addition to her own stories, Jennifer has illustrated books for many well-known authors, including Jill Paton Walsh, Floella Benjamin and Mary Hoffman. Her book with Mary Hoffman, *Nancy No-Size*, was also shortlisted for the Smarties Award. Her work has been televised in England and all over Europe on children's programmes, and in New Zealand and Australia. She wrote and illustrated *See You Later, Mum*, also published by Frances Lincoln.

To Nicola, Mark, Caroline and Phil – J.N.

This edition published in Great Britain in 2008 by
Frances Lincoln Children's Books, 4 Torriano Mews,
Torriano Avenue, London NW5 2RZ
www.franceslincoln.com

British Library Cataloguing in Publication Data available on request

ISBN 978-1-84507-895-9

Printed in Singapore

1 3 5 7 9 8 6 4 2

"Lucy! Did you pick all the flowers off my pansies?" asked Dad crossly.

Lucy and her cousin Alice were busy making decorations
for Lucy's mum's birthday tea that afternoon.

"Not us!" said Lucy. "We only picked one of each colour to put
in a bunch for Mum."

"Well, *someone* did," grumbled Dad, as he went inside.
"There isn't a single one left!"

It was very quiet in the garden. Just the snip of the scissors...
and a funny chomping sound.

"Alice!" said Lucy. "If you're eating sweets you should have shared!"

"I'm not. Look!" said Alice, opening her mouth wide.
"That's strange," said Lucy. "I'm not either."
But *something* was chomping.

Something in the flowerbed...

"Look," whispered Lucy. "That's what was chomping and what got
Dad's pansies. I'm going to catch her. I saw how on the telly once.
If you're very gentle and don't frighten them, it's easy."

But it wasn't so easy – the rabbit hopped this way and then that way,
humphing and snuffling crossly.

Alice and Lucy went this way and that, all over Dad's flowers.

"She sounds awfully grumpy," puffed Alice nervously. "Our neighbour's
rabbit bites. And scratches."

"Don't be upset, little bunny," said Lucy, wiggling a juicy dandelion
temptingly under the rabbit's nose. The rabbit stayed still a moment,
just long enough to sniff it. Just long enough for Lucy to sneak her hand
round behind the rabbit's ears and gently scoop her up.

Scrump, scrump, the rabbit calmly chewed up the dandelion.

"She's so silky soft," said Alice. "And look at her eyes –
they're like cherries. Do you think your mum and dad will let you keep her?"

"Mum might," said Lucy doubtfully. "She likes animals. But Dad won't be too keen on her if she eats up his plants. I wish I could keep her, though."

"I've got a brilliant idea," said Alice. "You could give her to your mum as a birthday present!"

"That's silly!" laughed Lucy. "Anyway, you're not supposed to give animals as presents in case people don't look after them properly.

But I know Mum does like rabbits – she used to have one called Billy when she was little…"

"So she'll like this one," said Alice persuasively.

"And if I help look after her and everything..." said Lucy.

They crept into the house and ran up to Lucy's bedroom. They put the rabbit on the bed, with a pillow on either side to keep her in.

"Quick, a box," said Lucy, "with lots of holes so she can breathe."

"Here's a good one," said Alice, tipping out the toybox on to the floor in a jumble.

"My animal face-paints!" cried Lucy. "I thought I'd lost them!"

"We could paint our faces to look like rabbits," said Alice, "with whiskers and everything! Here, paint my nose black."

"And we could do a play about a lost rabbit," said Lucy, "for my gran and your mum and dad at tea!"

Rip

Scrunch

After a while Lucy
remembered the real rabbit.

There was no sign of her.
But... there were plenty of
signs of where she had been!

"Oh, no!" groaned Lucy. "Where's she gone? That's spoilt the
surprise present!"

"Looks like the surprise present is doing the spoiling," said Alice.
"Your mum is going to have a fit."

"I'll have to wait till she's in a really good mood before I tell her,"
said Lucy miserably. "Dad gave her these slippers for Christmas and
she really likes them."

"She won't any more," said Alice.

They heard the doorbell ring and then voices downstairs.

"Look how you've grown, Laura!" Granny was saying to Lucy's little sister.

"Happy birthday!" Alice's mum and dad were saying to Lucy's mum.

"I've gone right off doing the play now," said Lucy.

So they cleaned up their faces and went slowly downstairs.
Lucy's dad had put up their special decorations and everyone
had brought lovely presents for Lucy's mum.

"Go on, tell her," whispered Alice, "she's in a good mood now."

"Mum," began Lucy, "you know I gave you my present this morning? Well, I had another one for you, only I can't find her. We had her upstairs, and we just took our eyes off her for one minute and she ran off!"

There was silence for a moment,
and then all the grown-ups burst out laughing.
"Did she hop away?" asked Alice's dad.
"Did she have long ears and a puffy tail?" asked Granny.
"How do you know?" asked Alice.

"Well, a rabbit hopped into the kitchen a while ago," explained Dad, "just as a lady came to the door, asking if we'd seen a rabbit because one of hers was missing. She said we could keep it if we wanted, because she had lots."

"What did you say?" asked Lucy anxiously.

"We were thinking of making it a surprise present for you," Dad continued. "We didn't know she was supposed to be a surprise present already! What made you think you could give something away that wasn't yours to give? Anyway, she's in an old box in the kitchen now."

"Oh, please can we keep her?" begged Lucy.
"You can have all my pocket money for the slipper
she chewed, and the rug was only old!"

"What slipper?" asked Mum.

"What rug?" asked Dad.

Everyone rushed into the kitchen. The box was there all right,
but it was… rabbit-less!

"Oh, dear," said Lucy in a small voice, "she must have got out again.
She's a bit of a naughty rabbit…"

"But she's very nice," added Alice quickly. "She just chews a lot."

"We can see that," said Alice's mum. "A world class champion chomper,
isn't she!"

"Hmmm," said Lucy's mum.

After a moment Mum said, "It's my birthday, so I'm not going to get upset. You'd better catch her right away. We *can* keep her, *but* the place for a rabbit, especially a naughty rabbit, is in the garden."

"In a nice roomy hutch in the garden," added Dad firmly,
"where she can run around but keep out of mischief.
We'll make her one after tea…"

. . . And that's what they did.